Fairy Realm

BOOK 2

The flower fairies

Fairy Realm

The flower fairies

BOOK 2

EMILY RODDA

ILLUSTRATIONS BY RAOUL VITALE

HARPERCOLLINS*PUBLISHERS*

Library of Congress Cataloging-in-Publication Data

Rodda, Emily.

  The flower fairies / Emily Rodda. — 1st American ed.

     p.   cm. — (Fairy realm ; #2)

  Originally published: Sydney, N.S.W. : ABC Books, 2000.

  Summary: Jessie returns to the magical world where her grandmother was born, where she deals with some griffins, dances with fairies, and borrows something to help her dance in her school concert.

  ISBN 0-06-009586-5 — ISBN 0-06-009587-3 (lib. bdg.)

  [1. Fairies—Fiction. 2. Griffins—Fiction. 3. Dance—Fiction. 4. Self-confidence—Fiction. 5. Fantasy.] I. Title.

PZ7.R5996 Fl 2003   2002017286

[Fic]—dc21   CIP

Typography by Karin Paprocki

7 8 9 10

❖

First American Edition

Previously published by ABC Books for the

AUSTRALIAN BROADCASTING CORPORATION

GPO Box 9994 Sydney NSW 2001

Originally published under the name

Mary-Anne Dickinson as the Storytelling Charms Series 1994

CONTENTS

CHAPTER ONE

The Trouble with Magic

J essie stepped through the door in the hedge that led to the secret garden and gasped in surprise. There, quietly nibbling at the grass, was Maybelle, the miniature horse from the fairy world of the Realm. Maybelle raised her head, and Jessie saw that the red ribbons in her mane were dusted with gold flecks of magic that twinkled in the early-morning sun.

"About time you turned up," the little horse said grumpily. "I've been hanging around here for ages!"

Jessie stared at her. "Have you?" she gulped at last.

Maybelle sniffed. "I need to talk to you, and I got tired of waiting for you to come over and see us," she said. "It's been weeks! Have you forgotten all about us?"

"Of course not!" exclaimed Jessie. "It's just that . . . I've been so busy."

Maybelle snorted. Obviously she couldn't imagine how anything could be as important as visiting the Realm.

But Jessie really had been busy. She'd been living at Blue Moon, her grandmother's big old house in the mountains, for six weeks now. There'd been a lot to do in that short time. She'd had to help Rosemary, her mother, pack up their house in the city, ready for the move. Then she'd had to help her unpack their clothes and other belongings and store them in the Blue Moon cupboards. Then the holidays had ended and she'd had to start at her new school.

For six weeks her mind had been full of work, plans and problems. She hadn't forgotten for a moment the amazing adventure that had made her new life possible, or the wonderful beings she'd met in the Realm.

How could she forget?

Six weeks ago, she'd discovered the magic Door to the Realm in the part of the Blue Moon grounds Granny called "the secret garden." She'd found out then that her grandmother, Jessica Belairs, wasn't what she seemed. Granny wasn't an ordinary human grandmother at all, but the true Queen of the Realm, one of the fairy Folk. She had left her world many years ago to marry the human man she loved. Now her sister Helena ruled in her place, but Granny still had her Queenly powers, as Jessie had seen with her own amazed eyes.

But Granny's secret wasn't something she talked about—even to Jessie. And with all the ordinary things Jessie had to think about, the magic world she'd entered through the secret garden had started to seem to her more and more like something in a story she'd read, or a film she'd seen, and less and less like a real place.

In fact, sometimes when she thought about it, she wondered if it had all been a dream. But then she'd look down at her wrist, at the chain bracelet hung with a gold heart charm that had been the Realm's gift to her. And she knew that the Realm had been no dream, and remembered that the bracelet was a promise that any time she wanted to, she could return.

She smiled at Maybelle. "What did you want to talk to me about?" she asked.

Maybelle pawed the grass with her front hoof. "I thought it was about time you came back to see us," she said. "The Realm's got shocking problems at the moment, and we could do with a hand."

"What shocking problems?" demanded Jessie. "Surely you've got all the magic you need now." She pointed. "More than enough, I'd say. You've got it all over your ribbons."

Maybelle snorted irritably and shook her mane so that flecks of gold flew into the air and whirled in the sunbeams. Jessie felt little thrills like tiny electric shocks as some of the shining specks fell on her skin. She shivered and giggled.

Maybelle glared at her. "Now don't you get silly too," she ordered. "I've got enough problems with that in the Realm. That's the trouble with magic.

There always seems to be too much of it, or too little. When you came to the Realm last time, we were running out of it, and thanks to you that problem was solved. But now we've got too much. And that's another problem altogether."

"Too much magic?" Jessie giggled again. She could still feel little thrills of excitement all over her arms and face. "How can there be too much magic?"

Maybelle sighed deeply. "They say it always happens just after the magic is renewed," she said. "There's an explosion of it, see, and then for ages afterwards the dust gets into everything. And everyone," she added darkly. "You should see Giff. That elf is just about uncontrollable. Silly as a wheel. And the flower fairies are worse than he is. They're not terribly sensible at the best of times, in my opinion. But now . . . hopeless!"

Jessie bit her lip to keep her giggles back, and nodded sympathetically.

"But the griffins are the real reason I've come to see you," Maybelle grumbled on. "They're the Queen's pets. And they're supposed to guard the

Realm's treasures. Well, that's fine. Let them guard the treasures. No one's arguing about that. But they're not supposed to get so full of themselves that they take over guarding everything else too. Are they?"

"I suppose not," Jessie murmured.

"I'd give anything for a bit of peace and quiet," Maybelle complained. "I'd like just for once to wake up in the morning without my mane and tail all full of giggling fairies. Just for once to have a quiet bowl of oats for breakfast, or a bit of sugar maybe, without having to fight some griffin to get it." She looked up. "You wouldn't by any chance have some sugar about you at the moment, would you?" she asked hopefully.

"No, sorry," said Jessie. "But I could go up to the house and get you some, if you like. Or some bread. Everything's still on the table from breakfast."

Maybelle licked her lips. "Thanks," she said. "Thanks for the offer. But on the whole I'd rather you just came through to the Realm with me right now and tried to sort the griffins out. You're good with magic. That was obvious last time. So—"

"But I'm *not* good with magic," cried Jessie. "Granny's the one who knows about it. She's the one who renewed the Realm's magic. All I did was bring her to you. And to do that I just used human common sense."

"Well, whatever you used, it worked," Maybelle said, nodding. "And I'd be very grateful if you'd stop arguing with me, and come and do it again!" She pursed her lips and tapped the ground with her hoof, waiting.

Jessie grinned. She really didn't think she'd be able to help Maybelle with her problem. But of course she was dying to have an excuse to visit the Realm again. And it *was* Saturday. There was nothing else she had to do, except clean up after breakfast. Mum and Granny had gone shopping and wouldn't be back for an hour or two. So why not?

That was one of the wonderful things about being at Blue Moon. Mum would never have left her alone in the house even for half an hour back in the city. There was so much freedom here! Peace and quiet, and freedom. Starting at a new school had been hard, but that was a small price to pay for living at Blue Moon.

A beautiful blue-and-black butterfly fluttered towards the rosemary bushes that grew around the small, square lawn of the secret garden. Jessie frowned. There was only one cloud in the clear sky of her life at the moment. And that butterfly had just reminded her of it. Tonight! she thought. The concert! Oh, if only I'd kept my big mouth shut! If only . . .

"Well?" Maybelle's impatient voice broke into her thoughts. "What do you say? Will you come? Will you come and deal with the griffins?"

Jessie tried to put her worries out of her mind. "Of course I will," she said. "I don't know if I can help. But I'd love to come."

"Right, then," said Maybelle with satisfaction. "Let's go!"

Jessie put her hand on the little horse's back and closed her eyes.

"Open!" called Maybelle. Jessie felt the cool breeze on her cheek that meant the magic Door was opening. Then, with a tingling of excitement, she felt herself slipping away from her own world and slipping again into the place where her grandmother had been born, and where she herself had had the biggest adventure of her life. The Realm.

Jessie opened her eyes. She was standing on the pebbly roadway beside the tall, glossy green hedge that marked the border of the fairy world. She turned around. The black arch that was the magic Door was already fading, and in a single blink it had disappeared. Her heart skipped a beat.

"Don't worry, now, will you," said Maybelle. "Things are different round here since the magic came back. You won't have any trouble getting home this time."

Jessie swallowed and nodded. She looked around. Everything looked very much as she remembered. The road, the hedge, the fields, a few trees and bushes. The palace, she knew, was just a little way off, behind a grove of trees.

But there were differences. For one thing, the light was bright, rich and golden. Even more golden than it had been the last time she was here. The leaves of the trees and bushes were rustling and the air was full of sound. A humming, twittering, singing sound. Jessie listened carefully. It wasn't just one sound, she decided. She was hearing thousands upon thousands of sounds that all blended into one.

"They never stop talking these days," grumbled Maybelle, flicking her ears forward. "Morning till night—chatter, chatter, chatter. It's enough to drive a horse crazy." She lifted her head. "Be quiet!" she bellowed.

There was dead silence. Then came a chorus of delighted squeaks and cries. The tree branches thrashed and tossed. And suddenly hundreds of tiny creatures with gossamer wings in every possible shade and color were bursting from their hiding places and swooping, in a giggling, excited cloud, around Jessie's head.

maybelle is Disgusted

"Jessie, Jessie, Jessie!" chattered the fairies. Jessie felt their tiny hands brushing her long red hair, twisting it into a hundred tangles. She laughed in delight and held out her arm. Most of the little creatures turned their heads away shyly and went on hovering just out of reach. But five of the more daring ones fluttered lightly onto her fingers and perched there, looking up at her with pretty, mischievous faces.

Jessie stared at them, fascinated. When they were darting and flying around in a crowd the fairies all looked alike to her, but now she could see that each one was different. Just like human beings, she thought.

"They're so beautiful!" she said to Maybelle.

Maybelle shook her mane. Three fairies clinging there were flung, giggling, into the air. "They're all right in their place, I suppose," she grumbled. "But the magic gets them all excited, and then they're a plain nuisance. Especially the five you've got there. They're the youngest, and the worst of the lot. A real gang of troublemakers."

Jessie looked again at the fairies on her fingers. They did seem smaller than the others. Obviously they were the best of friends, for they stood in a row, holding hands, opening and closing their wings. The one perched on her thumb was dark, with black hair and eyes. Her silky dress was purple and her wings were soft green.

"You look like a violet," smiled Jessie.

The fairy giggled, put her hand over her mouth, and glanced around at her friends.

"She *is* Violet," sang the fairy balancing on Jessie's first finger. She had a round face with a pointed chin, flyaway fair hair and a bright yellow dress and wings. Her voice was so tiny that Jessie could hardly hear it. "She's very shy," the yellow fairy said, nodding and smiling. "But I'm not."

"Oh, I can see that," Jessie answered. "And if your friend is Violet, would I be right in thinking you're Daffodil?"

"Yes I am!" squeaked the yellow fairy in delight.

"They're mainly flower fairies around here," said Maybelle, "and a few rainbow ones. They tend to cluster round the Doors, so they can get into your world more easily."

"They really come into our world?" asked Jessie. "But no one ever sees them!"

"Oh, of course they see them," said Maybelle carelessly. "Especially now that the magic has been renewed. There's been a lot of to-ing and fro-ing lately. But most people in your world don't believe in fairies, and don't expect to see them, do they? So they don't notice them. It's as simple as that."

"Sometimes they see us and they say, 'A lot of butterflies about today, aren't there?'" burst out Daffodil. "We fool them!" She squeezed Violet's hand and they both broke into peals of laughter that sounded to Jessie like the ringing of tiny bells.

"We fool them!" echoed the fairy on Daffodil's other side, jumping up and down on her toes. Jessie looked at her closely. She had curly light brown hair. Her soft cheeks were pink, her flounced, frilled dress and curved wings were palest pink too, and a thin green sash was tied around her waist. Rose, thought Jessie. A pink rose.

"Don't you be too cocky, you young fairies," Maybelle warned them. "Don't forget, this is your first season out. There are lots of dangers outside the Doors. You two especially," she added, frowning at the fairies on Jessie's last two fingers.

One of them was dark and short-haired, with a starchy white dress and round yellow wings. The other had a long brown plait and was dressed all in blue.

They had been whispering and giggling together, and now they sighed and looked at each other. "No, Maybelle," they chorused. By the look of their cheeky expressions and rolling eyes, thought Jessie, they had no intention of following the little horse's good advice.

"What are your names?" she asked.

They jumped guiltily and fluttered their wings. "Daisy and Bluebell, miss," they said together.

"Oh, you don't have to call me 'miss,'" exclaimed Jessie, laughing in surprise. "It makes me feel like a teacher at school. Just call me Jessie."

Daisy and Bluebell beamed at her.

"Don't you go encouraging them," urged Maybelle. "They'll start hanging round you, and they'll cause you nothing but trouble."

"I think they're really sweet!" said Jessie. "I don't see how they could cause me any trouble at all!" She winked at the five fairies on her hand. "You're always welcome to visit me," she told them. "Any time you like!"

Maybelle grunted. "Well, don't say I didn't warn you," she said shortly. "Now, are you going to come with me and see about these griffins?"

The fairies had been whispering together. Now Daffodil, who seemed to have been chosen to speak for all of them, fluttered her wings and coughed politely. Jessie bent down to listen to her.

"It's our turn to dance in the ring soon. Would

17

you come and dance with us . . . Jessie?" the little fairy asked.

Jessie caught her breath. She felt herself blushing. "Oh . . . no . . . I can't do that," she said. She saw Daffodil's face fall and felt sorry. "It's just that I'm not very good at dancing, actually," she stammered.

Daffodil's face cleared. "Oh," she said, nodding wisely. She looked around at the others. "Jessie can't dance," she said loudly. "Remember we learned that some humans are like that?"

All five fairies peered curiously up at Jessie's face. She blushed more deeply.

"You'll be with us," called Daisy. "So you don't have to be shy, Jessie. There's no such thing as not being able to dance here."

"Jessie, come on!" snapped Maybelle. "There are more important things than—"

"Oh, please!" squeaked Daisy, jiggling excitedly.

"Please, please, please!" begged the others. And all the fairies darting around nearby took up the call. "Please, Jessie! Please, please, please!" The golden air rang with their tiny voices. The sound went on and on. Jessie looked around helplessly.

"Quiet!" bellowed Maybelle, swishing her tail.

There was another moment's stunned silence.

"Look, you've got to leave Jessie alone now," the little horse said firmly. "She's got something important to do with me. But I promise I'll bring her along to the dance after that. All right?" The fairies nodded, peeping at her with bright eyes. "All right. Now, scat!" Maybelle snorted violently, so that Violet, Daffodil, Rose, Daisy and Bluebell were blown, somersaulting and shrieking, off Jessie's fingers. "Again! Again!" they begged, jumping up and down in the air.

"Come on," ordered Maybelle, nudging Jessie's arm and moving off. Obediently, Jessie followed her, turning one last time to wave good-bye to the fairies who hovered like a cloud of butterflies behind her.

She was pleased to see that Maybelle was trotting in the direction of the trees that clustered in front of the palace. Maybe she'd see her old friends, Giff the elf and Patrice the palace housekeeper. Maybe she'd even see Queen Helena, who'd promised her a new charm for her bracelet every time she came to the Realm. Still, she thought, I mightn't have time. I don't think Maybelle will let me talk to anyone else till I've dealt with the griffins. Whatever griffins are. And then I've got to go to this dance thing.

Jessie sighed. Imagine running into a problem here just like the one she had at home! Her mind went back to that day in the classroom, in her first week at her new school. She'd still been feeling a bit lost and confused. She'd been sitting at her table with a few other kids, trying not to draw attention to herself, just minding her own business. And then . . .

". . . the spring concert," the teacher, Ms. Hewson, was saying, pushing back her curly hair and adjusting her glasses, "is only six weeks away. Now . . ." She consulted the list in her hand. "The sun. Who would like . . . ?"

Several hands shot up, including two at Jessie's table. "Right then—ah, Sal. You haven't been the sun before, have you? Good. Now—breeze?" More hands shot up. "Yes, Michael. Fine." Ms. Hewson made a note, and beamed. "Rabbits?" There was a groan. No one wanted to be a rabbit. Ms. Hewson sighed and made a note. "Rain? Flowers?" Hands went up all over the classroom.

Jessie looked round in confusion. It must be some sort of concert they had every year. Maybe she'd better volunteer for something. She didn't want Ms. Hewson to think she wasn't willing. And she certainly didn't want to end up being a rabbit.

"Butterfly?" sang Ms. Hewson, looking at the class over her glasses. That sounded okay. Jessie put up her hand. So did Irena Bins, whose family lived in the house next door to Blue Moon. Even though they were neighbors, Irena wasn't particularly friendly. She stuck to her own group and had hardly spoken to Jessie since she started at school.

"Ah, Jessie!" smiled Ms. Hewson. "That's nice. Well, Irena, I think we should give Jessie the part, don't you? You were the butterfly last year."

Irena looked sulky. Obviously she didn't agree.

"There's still the rainbow, Irena," soothed Ms. Hewson. "You'd do that awfully well, I think. Will I put you down for that?"

Irena tossed her glossy ponytail and said nothing.

"It doesn't matter, Ms. Hewson," babbled Jessie, feeling herself growing hot. "I don't mind."

"No, no," pronounced Ms. Hewson firmly. "Fair's fair. And Irena mustn't be a bad sport." She wrote on her pad. "Now. Jessie, butterfly; Irena, rainbow. Who would like to do the moon this year?"

And that was how it had happened. It wasn't until later that Jessie found out what a terrible mistake she'd made.

giff's retreat

Jessie folded her arms across her chest as she followed Maybelle into the grove of pale-leaved trees. She was remembering the lunch break that had followed Ms. Hewson's giving out of the parts for the spring concert.

Irena sat on a wooden seat, surrounded by her friends and shooting furious looks in Jessie's direction.

"Don't worry about her!" Sal, who sat at Jessie's table and had been chosen to be the sun, came up to Jessie. "Irena Bins always thinks she should be the star."

Jessie looked at her. She'd liked Sal as soon as she saw her on the first day. She had a really friendly face. There was a gap between her two front teeth, and she had freckles on her nose. Jessie thought she'd be perfect as the sun. She was warm and open, with a big, big smile. And she was smiling now. But her words sent a small chill down Jessie's spine.

"The butterfly isn't the star part, is it?" Jessie asked, as casually as she could.

Sal laughed. "Oh, of course it is," she said. "Didn't you know? Irena did it last year. And she was so stuck up about it, honestly!" She lowered her voice. "On a notice board in her room," she whispered, "she's got a big photograph of herself in her butterfly costume. Her father took the picture. And you know what she's got stuck around it?"

Jessie shook her head.

"Butterflies," said Sal. "Poor dead butterflies. All different kinds she's caught. She doesn't know what sorts of butterflies they are, or anything. She just wants a pretty frame for her own picture.

26

I think she's really off."

Jessie glanced at Irena. She felt a bit guilty for whispering about her with Sal. But since Irena had obviously decided that Jessie was her enemy, maybe it was wise to find out a bit about her.

"She was sure she'd get the part again this year," Sal went on. "She thinks she's so great. But I don't think she's such an amazing dancer, anyway."

The small chill running down Jessie's spine became a stream of ice. "Dancer?" she echoed weakly.

"You're so lucky you can dance," Sal rattled on. "I did ballet for two terms when I was younger, but I was hopeless, and Mum let me stop."

She sighed with satisfaction while Jessie gulped and wondered what on earth she was going to do. "That's why being the sun's good," Sal said. "You just get to stand round at the back holding out your arms. I'd be absolutely petrified if I had to do a dance on my own in front of everyone, like you."

By this time Jessie's heart had sunk to the soles of her shoes. She couldn't dance! She'd never had a single proper ballet lesson. Only some creative-movement-to-music classes at her old school. And the special teacher who'd come in to teach those classes had made it very clear that Jessie's efforts to move her thin arms and legs in time to the music were not a bit creative, let alone graceful. She winced as if she was in pain every time it was Jessie's turn to dance. And of course that made Jessie even more embarrassed and stiff. As the lessons went on, she'd got worse instead of better. Now just the thought of dancing made her freeze up.

The one good thing to come out of that terrible lunch break was that Sal had asked Jessie to come and eat with her and her group under the oak tree at the end of the school yard. After two days of lonely lunches, it was nice to have company. But as Jessie sat with her new friends and listened to the gossip and talk about the play and the parts they were all going to be practicing for the next six weeks, she felt sick.

It was going to be so awful to have to admit she couldn't take the butterfly part after all. She imagined Irena's mouth pursing smugly as she leaned over to whisper behind her hand to the person sitting next to her. She imagined Sal's cheerful face falling in surprise and disappointment.

But as it happened, she didn't have to disappoint Sal. Not like that, anyway. Because when she went in to see Ms. Hewson after school to explain, Ms. Hewson had looked at her over her glasses, smiled very kindly, and refused even to consider letting her give up the butterfly part.

"You don't need to have done ballet to do the dance, Jessie," she said. "It's very, very simple. Most of it you just make up yourself, as you go along. You'll be absolutely fine. All you have to do is move gracefully to the music."

Move gracefully to the music! That was exactly what Jessie couldn't do. And the next few weeks' practices had proved it too.

Everyone else slowly learned their parts. Gradually the play came together. But Jessie, who only had to flutter around and didn't even have to remember proper dance steps, was awkward and shy. Her costume was good. She was wearing a black leotard and tights, and had silver antennae on her head and floating sky-blue wings. But she was a hopeless butterfly. She knew it, and so did everyone else.

"That was very nice, Jessie. You look beautiful. But on the night, just try to forget yourself and move with the music," Ms. Hewson had said after Friday's dress rehearsal, the last before the concert on Saturday night. "Just think, 'I'm a beautiful, graceful butterfly,' and enjoy yourself!" She said the same thing every time, and she always said it kindly, with a smile on her face. But Jessie could tell she was terribly disappointed and worried.

"That Jessie dances more like a stick insect than a butterfly, if you ask me," Irena Bins muttered to one of her friends. "She'll ruin the whole thing!"

"Your costume is so lovely," said Sal loyally, as they walked home. "Who made your wings?"

"My grandmother made them for my mother when she was a fairy in a play years ago," Jessie answered.

She remembered how Granny had gone look-ing for the wings and found them in an old chest of drawers in the storeroom, wrapped in tissue paper. She remembered how Granny had smiled as she handed them to her. "Your mother always loved to dance," she said. "And so did I. We're so proud of you, Jessie."

After that, Jessie just couldn't tell her how she felt. But tonight Granny would see what a bad dancer she was. And so would Mum. And everyone else. Irena Bins was right. Jessie would ruin the whole spring concert.

No wonder the brightness of her first weeks in her new home had been clouded. No wonder she hadn't even tried to visit the Realm again. Even now, walking on its soft grass, breathing in its golden air, the thought of the play was filling her mind and stopping her from enjoying herself.

"Oh dear," sighed Jessie aloud.

Maybelle stopped and looked around at her. "What's up with you?" she inquired.

"It's just . . . oh, nothing," said Jessie. She looked ahead, and her heart gave a skip as she saw Queen Helena's golden palace shining between the trees. She'd been so busy thinking that she hadn't noticed where Maybelle was leading her.

"Are we going to the palace?" she asked hopefully. Suddenly she'd had a marvelous idea. She would ask Queen Helena to help her with the butterfly dance. Perhaps the Queen could put some sort of spell on her.

Maybelle shook her head. "Not the palace itself. Round the back," she said. "The food storehouse. First things first, I say. We're nearly there. Just around this—" She jumped violently as there was a sharp explosion above their heads.

"Look out below!" squeaked a voice from the trees. "Oh no! *E-e-eek!*"

There was a smashing, cracking sound. A shrieking bundle of green, a trailing rope, bells, streamers, a mosquito net, an old shawl, a sun hat, a rusty door-knocker and two broken shopping baskets crashed to the ground.

Jessie and Maybelle jumped aside just in time.

"Giff!" roared Maybelle at the groaning green heap lying in the mess on the ground beside them. "What on earth do you think you're playing at? You could have crushed us to smithereens."

Giff the elf sat up slowly, his long, pointed

ears bent nearly double. In one hand he held a piece of string to which was tied a tattered bit of green rubber. In the other he held a notice. *Giff's Retreat*, it read.

He looked at the notice and began to cry. "Oh, my beautiful new house," he wept. "It's ruined! That stupid balloon . . ."

"What new house?" shouted Maybelle. "Giff, you absurd elf, why are you making a new house? You've got a nice house already."

Giff wiped his nose with a green-spotted handkerchief and stood up. "Haven't you heard?" he sniffed. "A griffin's decided to guard my house. And it won't let me in. I've been sleeping on Patrice's couch for three days, waiting for it to go, but it won't. So I decided . . ." Then he noticed Jessie. "Jessie!" he squealed. He dropped the string and the notice and flew into her arms.

Jessie laughed. It was so good to see him!

Giff started to tell her about the house he'd been trying to build. A griffin was guarding the hardware storehouse, he said, so he hadn't been able to get any nails or proper wood or anything. But he'd gathered a few bits and pieces from Patrice's junk room, and he'd planned to make a really sweet little house out of those. It was to be suspended by a balloon, right at the top of a tree. His plans had worked perfectly—at first. But then he'd decided to nail his *Giff's Retreat* sign to the balloon. Things went from bad to worse after that.

"Poor Giff!" said Jessie, shaking her head and trying not to let him see her smile.

Giff snuffled again. "So I *still* haven't anywhere to live," he moaned. "And I'm tired of sleeping on Patrice's couch. It's got lumps! And Maybelle doesn't care. She doesn't care that I'm homeless. She doesn't care that the griffins—"

"I'll have you know, Giff," Maybelle broke in sternly, "that I've brought Jessie to the Realm especially to do something about the griffins. We're going to the food storehouse first. If you want to come with us, come. If you don't, stay where you are. Just don't hold us up. There've been enough delays already!"

Giff meekly took Jessie's hand and the three friends trudged on through the trees until they reached the palace. As they began walking around to the back of the building, Jessie remembered what she'd been thinking about before Giff had dropped so surprisingly out of the sky.

"Maybelle, could I see Queen Helena, do you think?" she said. "I've got something to ask her."

The little horse grunted. "Sorry, didn't I tell you?" she answered. "Queen Helena's off traveling with the King and Princess Christie—visiting the people and creatures in all the different parts of the Realm. Celebrating the renewal of the magic. That's the whole point, you see. The griffins wouldn't be a problem if it wasn't for that. Queen Helena can manage them. They are her pets, after all."

Jessie felt bitterly disappointed. What bad luck! Queen Helena could have helped her with her butterfly dance. She was sure of that.

They pushed through some bushes and came out behind the palace and in front of a tall, round building made of stone. Suddenly there was a deafening, screeching roar. And in an instant Jessie had forgotten all about school, and Ms. Hewson, and Irena Bins. And she'd forgotten about the butterfly dance.

Because she was staring straight at the slashing claws and wicked curved beak of a huge, angry, winged monster.

CHAPTER FOUR

The Griffin

Jessie screamed. Giff screamed. Even Maybelle snuffled through her nose in shock and took a quick step backward. "Run for the bushes!" she ordered. "It won't follow us there."

They scuttled back to the shelter of the bushes beside the palace and crouched there, panting.

"What is it?" cried Jessie, peering out in horror at the savage creature lumbering backward and forward in front of the storehouse, flapping its wings, lashing its tail and snapping its beak. Its back legs and tail were like a lion's. But its head and claws were those of a huge eagle.

Maybelle stared at her. "You know what that is, Jessie. What's the matter with you? That's a griffin."

"*That's* a griffin?" Jessie exclaimed. "But . . . but it's *horrible*. It's *terrifying*! It . . . it wants to *eat* us!"

"Yes," agreed Maybelle calmly. "That's the trouble with griffins."

"But you told me they were Queen Helena's *pets*!" Jessie shook her head. "No, no. I'm sorry, but I can't help you after all." She caught sight of Giff's surprised and disappointed face. "I—I was expecting something . . . smaller," she explained. "Something without a terrible beak and claws. And with a nicer nature."

"Well, if they were smaller and weren't so nasty we could deal with them ourselves, Jessie," snapped Maybelle.

"Or even if there weren't so *many* of them," added Giff gloomily.

"How many are there?" asked Jessie, staring in fascinated horror at the creature, which was now sitting scratching like a dog.

"Four," sighed Maybelle. "There were two, but

they had twin griffinettes a couple of years ago. And Queen Helena, well, she's so soft-hearted . . ."

"Too soft-hearted!" snuffled Giff.

"Yes, well, maybe. Anyway, she couldn't bring herself to give the griffinettes away, so she kept them. And now they're almost as big as their parents, and just as much trouble."

"Psst!" The piercing whisper right behind her ear nearly made Jessie jump out of her skin. She twisted around quickly to meet the black button eyes and plump face of Patrice, the palace housekeeper.

"Jessie," exclaimed Patrice, "what on earth are you doing here?" She turned and frowned at Maybelle. "You brought her, didn't you?" she demanded, shaking her finger at the tiny horse.

Maybelle flicked her tail. "Someone had to do something!" she snorted. "I need my oats."

"Oh, you and your oats!" hissed Patrice, glancing nervously at the griffin. "At least you can eat grass. What about food for everyone else? And what about the hardware storehouse? No one can build anything, or make anything.

And what about Giff's house?"

"Yes! What about that?" echoed Giff mournfully.

Maybelle wrinkled her nose and huffed. "Oh yes, all that too," she said.

Over by the food storehouse, the griffin grumbled to itself and settled down by the door. But its glowing eyes still darted suspiciously around, watching for the slightest movement.

"Let me get this straight," said Jessie. "There are four griffins. One's here, at the food storehouse. One's at the hardware storehouse. And one's at Giff's house. Where's the other one?"

"It's at the treasure house, where it belongs," said Patrice. "Where they *all* belong. They've gone crazy with all this magic in the air, and they've decided between themselves that they're not all needed at the treasure house any more. So three of them have gone off and found other places to guard. That's all griffins know about—guarding things. No one can reason with them."

"No one ever could, except Queen Helena," said Maybelle gloomily.

"Well, you'll have to send for her, then," said Jessie reasonably. "She'll have to come back from her trip."

"She can't!" moaned Patrice, twisting her apron. "She's only halfway around the Realm. The magic's just been renewed. It's a great celebration here. She can't disappoint half her subjects like that."

"Well, she'll be pretty disappointed herself if she comes back and finds that everyone at home's dead of hunger or been eaten by griffins, won't she?" Jessie pointed out. "I really think you'd better send for her."

"It's just . . ." Maybelle rolled her eyes and sighed. "It's just that I thought maybe you could think of a way to save us having to do that. We hate to worry her. Still, if you won't . . ."

"It's not that I won't!" exclaimed Jessie, more loudly than she'd meant. She saw the griffin turn its fiery gaze toward the bushes. She lowered her voice. "It's not that I won't. It's that I *can't*, Maybelle."

Maybelle sighed again. And Giff sighed too. His ears were drooping nearly down to his shoulders.

Jessie bit her lip. "Look," she said. "I'll think about it. Maybe I can come up with some plan or other."

"Jessie, Jessie, Jessie!" sang dozens of tiny, tinkling voices from the grove of trees behind them. Maybelle groaned. "Not those pests again," she muttered.

A crowd of fairies flew out from their shelter, hovered over Jessie's head for a moment and then darted off, laughing. They were heading straight for the griffin.

The beast raised its terrible eyes to look at the delicate creatures fluttering around its head. Jessie clapped her hand over her mouth. "Oh! Look out!" she called.

Patrice beamed. "Don't fret, dearie. The griffins won't touch the flower fairies. I think they sort of like them, really. If griffins can like anyone."

"Jessie, Jessie, Jessie," chorused the fairies, leaping in the air and bouncing on the griffin's wings. "Come on! Come on! Come on!"

"Pests!" snapped Maybelle.

"Dear little things," smiled Patrice. "Do they

44

want you to dance with them, Jessie? I'll bet they do. They miss Queen Helena and Christie terribly, poor loves."

Jessie squirmed uncomfortably. "I can't dance, Patrice. They wouldn't have any fun dancing with me. They'd just be embarrassed."

"Oh, I wouldn't worry about that," said Patrice. "I don't think flower fairies know how to be embarrassed. They'll have plenty of fun." She looked sharply into Jessie's face. "You look as though you could do with a bit of fun yourself," she added. "You feeling a bit peaky?"

Jessie shook her head. She didn't want to talk about her problem. Not now.

"Well," said Patrice, after a moment, "there's not much point in hiding out here, is there? If you're going to do some thinking, dearie, you may as well come into the palace and do it there. Besides, if you're going to dance with the little ones afterward, we'll have to go to Queen Helena's bedroom so I can get you some wings."

Jessie's eyes widened. "Wings?" she exclaimed.

"A waste of time," snorted Maybelle.

"Nonsense," Patrice snorted back. "For all you know, Maybelle, the dancing will help Jessie think. Stir up her brains, or something."

"Or something," repeated Giff, nodding eagerly.

"Follow me," said Patrice.

Giff slipped his hand into Jessie's. "Do you think the dance will really stir up your brains?" he asked.

Jessie had to smile. "I hope so, Giff," she said. She turned to follow Patrice and Maybelle. All the time one word was ringing in her ears. *Wings*.

Jessie stood, amazed, in the center of Queen Helena's beautiful bedroom. It was large and light. Long, transparent curtains billowed at the windows. The soft white carpet was scattered with tiny yellow flowers and green leaves.

But it wasn't the pretty carpet or the delicate furniture that Jessie was gasping at now. She was staring at Patrice, who had opened a large carved chest at the end of the bed and was carefully laying out its contents on the yellow silk bedcover.

Wings. Shining, shimmering wings.

"Come closer, dearie," called Patrice, beckoning. "You'd better choose for yourself."

Jessie tiptoed over to the bed. The wings lay spread out on the yellow silk. They looked as if they would tear at the slightest touch.

"Oh, I don't think I should," Jessie stammered. "Queen Helena wouldn't like it. They look so precious."

"They are precious," Patrice agreed, smoothing a fold from the edge of a wing with one gentle brown finger. "But they're stronger than they look, dearie. You won't hurt them. And I know Queen Helena would want you to borrow a pair. She'd love the idea of the flower fairies having a big person to dance with while she's away. They do adore it, bless their hearts. And none of the Folk here will dance without Helena, you see. It's not done. It's bad manners, in the Realm."

"But it would be all right for me?" asked Jessie.

"Oh, yes, of course! Because you're a human, aren't you, dearie? The rules don't apply to you. Now. Which pair would you like?"

CHAPTER FIVE

The plan

J essie looked carefully at the wings. There were dozens of them, and they were all different. She saw that they were exactly the same shape as the ones her grandmother had given her for the butterfly dance. But Granny's wings had been hemmed on the sewing machine and made of ordinary silk. These seemed to have been made with no thread at all, and the material was like nothing Jessie had ever seen or felt. They were all so beautiful! It was impossible to choose between them.

"I have some wings at home that Granny made," she said, her eyes darting from one glorious color to the next. "They're the same shape as these. But . . ."

Patrice's button eyes softened. "Ah, yes," she said. "Well, of course your grandmother would have remembered the design, wouldn't she? She'd have chosen from this chest of wings many times, as a girl. The Folk always wear them when they dance with the flower and rainbow fairies. And your grandmother danced often. She was a princess, remember. The princess who was going to be Queen one day. Besides, she adored dancing." Again the plump little housekeeper smoothed a wing lovingly.

"But she couldn't make wings like these in your world, dearie," she explained. "To make wings like these you need Realm magic. As I said, they're precious."

Precious. Jessie stood quite still, staring at the wings. She'd had an idea. An idea that might solve all the Realm's problems with the griffins. She thought about it with growing excitement. It just might work! It was certainly worth a try.

"Come on, Jessie," urged Patrice. "You have to

choose. Maybelle will be having conniptions in my kitchen if we don't get on. The best rule, they say, is to choose the wings you feel are most like you."

Jessie decided not to say anything to Patrice about her idea yet. She'd wait until she could talk to Maybelle as well.

But before she could do that, she had to make a choice. She looked over all the wings again. Her hand stretched out and hovered over a yellow pair that shimmered pink at the edges like a rose, or a sunset. Then it moved to a creamy white pair that shone blue and purple and green like the inside of a shell as it caught the light. Still she hesitated.

Her eyes moved over the rich colors. Pink, lilac, soft grey with silver stars, rich purple veined and edged in gold, buttery yellow, palest green . . . And then she saw them, over on one side. Her wings. Pure sky blue, deepening to richer blue at the bottom, fading to lilac at the top. Very like the ones Granny had made for Mum all those years ago. She pointed. "I'll have those, please," she said.

Patrice beamed. "They were your grandmother's favorite," she said. "She wore these far more than any of the others. Isn't it lovely that you chose those?" She picked up the wings. "Turn around, dearie, and I'll put them on for you."

Jessie turned around as Patrice fastened the center of the shining wings to the back of her top, and slipped the fine bands at the tips around each of her wrists. She was glad she had worn a skirt today instead of jeans. She raised her arms and gasped with pleasure as the movement made the wings flutter around her. They felt wonderful. They made her feel quite different. Lighter than air. She spun round to look at herself in the long mirror that stood by the windows.

"That's the way, dearie," said Patrice with an approving look. "Now . . ."

But then Jessie squeaked with shock. She was staring at the mirror. "P-Patrice!" she stuttered. "L-look at me!"

Patrice frowned slightly. "Something wrong?" she asked.

Jessie raised her arms again, her mouth gaping, her eyes wide with excitement as she watched her reflection. The beautiful blue wings were shimmering behind her, her skirt billowed in the breeze from the open windows, her long red hair was lifting and falling, and her feet — her feet were trailing high above the carpet!

"Patrice," she gasped. "I'm floating! Patrice! I'm . . . I'm flying!"

Patrice laughed. "Of course, dearie," she said. "What did you expect?"

In a happy dream Jessie half walked, half flew back to Patrice's cozy kitchen on the ground floor of the palace.

Maybelle and Giff were waiting for her impatiently.

"At last!" exclaimed Maybelle. She watched Jessie turning and twisting in the air and huffed crossly. "Now she's gone silly!" she complained to Patrice. "She'll be no use whatever to us now, thanks to you."

"Oh, never mind all that," smiled Patrice, getting out some glasses and putting ice into them. "Doesn't she remind you of her grandmother? See, she chose the wings Jessica used to wear. Isn't that lovely?"

Giff sniffled. "Lovely," he repeated. He pulled out his handkerchief and blew his nose. "It makes me sad."

"It makes me happy!" cried Jessie, spinning around the kitchen table.

Maybelle tapped her hoof on the floor. "Any thoughts on the griffin question?" she inquired.

Jessie stopped sailing around the room. In the excitement of flying, she'd actually forgotten all about her idea and the griffins! She sat down at the table. "I have had a thought, actually," she said.

Patrice put a tall, frosted glass of rosy pink drink in front of her. "I don't have any chocolate left, dearie," she said. "I was going to try to bully that griffin into letting me get some, and a few other things I'm out of, when I bumped into you. So I can't make you hot chocolate like last time. But I think you'll like this. Have a taste."

Jessie sipped. The drink was wonderful! It was—well, she didn't know how to describe the taste. It was cool, and very refreshing. It wasn't sour and it wasn't sugary. It was a bit like raspberry lemonade might be, but without the fizz. And it left a tingle on her tongue after she'd swallowed, like sherbet did. She licked her lips and took another drink.

"Your idea!" urged Maybelle. "Tell!"

"The griffins' proper job is to guard the treasure house. Right?" Jessie began.

Giff nodded violently and gulped his drink.

"But because they've been affected by all the magic floating around, they've suddenly decided that only one of them is really needed to guard the treasure house," Jessie went on. "So that means that three of them are free to go off and find other places to guard. They don't care that no one wants them to. All they know is that their job is to guard things, so they find whatever they can that looks important and they guard that."

"We know!" groaned Giff. "We know!"

"My idea," said Jessie slowly, "is to persuade the griffins that they're all needed back at the treasure house. Then they'll leave the other places alone."

"How will we do that, though?" asked Patrice anxiously. "How do we persuade them?"

55

"Simple. We let them know that something very precious to Queen Helena has to be guarded," said Jessie. "Something that's not usually kept in the treasure house but is about to be moved there."

"Something precious?" asked Giff. "What do we have that's precious?"

"The wings," said Jessie. "Queen Helena's chest of wings."

There was a short silence. Maybelle, Patrice and Giff looked at one another. Then Maybelle spoke. "It could work, you know," she said. "Everyone knows how much Queen Helena cares about the wings. Even the griffins know. But the problem is, how do we get close enough to them to make them understand? They just screech and carry on as soon as they see us."

"I've thought of that, too," said Jessie.

They listened carefully while she explained. And then they began to smile.

CHAPTER SIX

At the Treasure House

The treasure house wasn't really a house at all, Jessie found. It was an underground room at one side of the palace. All you could see above the ground was a huge flat stone covered with strange carvings. On each side of the stone was a small tree with red leaves. And on top of the stone crouched a fearsome-looking griffin.

"It's much bigger than the one guarding the food storehouse," whispered Jessie nervously, peering out at it from the corner of the palace building.

"Oh yes," Patrice said, nodding. "It's the daddy

of the family. Huge, isn't it?"

"Huge!" echoed Giff, twisting his handkerchief.

Jessie glanced behind her at the two rows of palace guards waiting there with the chest of wings. They were standing at attention, in full uniform, but their faces were worried.

"Get ready," she breathed. The leader nodded.

Jessie looked down at her hand, where Violet, Daffodil, Rose, Daisy and Bluebell were jumping up and down with impatience.

"Okay?" she whispered. "Remember everything?" The fairies nodded.

"Go, then," said Jessie, raising her hand. And immediately the five tiny figures darted from her fingers and sped, chattering and laughing, to perch on one of the red trees right beside the griffin's left ear.

The griffin raised its head and rumbled thoughtfully in its throat, but made no attempt to scare the fairies away.

"Did you hear about Queen Helena's precious chest of wings?" squeaked Daisy at the top of her voice. "Did you hear that it has to be moved from her room because the room is to be painted?"

"Yes! I heard!" shouted Bluebell. "But, um, oh dear, Daisy! I'm *so-o* worried. The wings are Queen Helena's *greatest* treasure. However are they going to be kept safe *now*?"

Jessie covered her face with her hands. "Oh no," she said in a low voice. "I'm not sure this is going to work. The fairies aren't very good at acting, are they?"

Maybelle snorted. "Don't worry about that," she said. "Griffins are pretty stupid. Look, it's listening to them."

Sure enough, the griffin had turned its head toward the fairies.

"Before she went away, Queen Helena told the guards that when the time came they had to bring the wings here, to the treasure house," said Daffodil, loudly and slowly. "She thought that there would be *four* strong griffins to guard them here, and they would be safe. But only *one* griffin is here to guard them now. And if an enemy comes . . ."

There was silence. Jessie saw Daffodil dig Rose sharply in the ribs. Rose jumped. "Oh," she shrieked. "Oh, yes, um . . . If an *enemy* comes, *one* griffin might not be enough. And if even a *single* pair of wings is stolen, poor Queen Helena will be so, *so* unhappy."

The griffin stayed quite still. Its brow wrinkled. It looked as though it was thinking about what the fairies had said—although, Jessie admitted to herself, it was hard to tell. It could just have had a pain in the stomach.

Violet clasped her hands and took a deep breath. "I wish *all* the griffins were here to guard the wings," she bellowed. "Don't you?"

"Oh yes, yes!" shouted all the fairies together. "If only *all* the griffins were here to guard the chest of wings! Then it would be safe, just as Queen Helena had planned."

Daffodil cupped her hand around her ear. "Listen!" she yelled. "I think I can hear some guards coming with the chest right now!"

Jessie crossed her fingers. She turned to the leader of the guards and gave a signal.

At a nod from their leader, four of the guards picked up the chest by its handles. The others formed lines on either side. Then they smartly marched around the corner of the palace, toward the treasure house.

As soon as it saw them, the griffin sprang to its feet, its red eyes blazing.

The leader of the guards cleared her throat and stepped forward, spreading out a paper she held in her hand.

"By order, a chest of wings to be placed for safety in the royal treasure house," she read in a ringing voice, and flung open the chest to show its glimmering contents.

The griffin glared. It held the guard's gaze for a long moment. Then it threw back its head and let forth a blood-curdling shriek. The red trees quivered and a few leaves fell to the ground. The five flower fairies clung desperately to their perches. The guards rocked back on their heels in shock but stood their ground.

Jessie grabbed Patrice's hand.

"It's going to eat the guards," moaned Giff. "Oh it is, I know it!"

The griffin screeched again. And this time its

call was answered. From three different places.

"It's calling its family!" Maybelle burst out in a piercing whisper.

A terrifying rush of sound filled their ears. They looked up. The three other griffins were flying toward the treasure house, their wings beating the air, their sharp curved beaks gaping open. They wheeled in the air and plunged earthward, landing beside the flat stone.

Now the guards were facing four angry-looking creatures. Still they held their ground, standing to attention around the precious chest.

The father griffin moved slowly from the top of the flat stone. It fixed the head guard with a steady, serious gaze, and sat down deliberately in front of one of the red trees. The biggest of the other griffins lumbered over to join it. The other two took up their positions on the opposite side.

The head guard saluted. Only a slight sheen of sweat on her top lip showed how nervous she was. She shut the lid of the chest and pointed at the flat stone, murmuring some words Jessie couldn't hear.

With a grating sound the stone slid backward,

revealing a wide, steep stairway. The leader of the guards nodded, and the four guards carrying the chest stepped forward. Followed by their leader, they marched to the stairway and then, slowly and carefully, began to ease the chest down the stairs into the darkness below. After a few moments the sounds of their footsteps died away. The griffins sat as still as if they were carved in stone.

In the ten minutes it took for the guards to return, Jessie, Patrice and Giff gripped one another's hands in silence. Even the flower fairies were still and watchful. The guards remaining by the treasure house stood to attention, looking straight ahead.

At last, to Jessie's enormous relief, they heard again the sound of footsteps on the stairs. The five guards climbed back up into the sunlight, blinking. Without looking at the griffins, they marched briskly across the grass to join the rest of the troop, while behind them the stone slid slowly back into position.

Jessie breathed out. It seemed to her that she'd been holding her breath for a very long time.

The head guard faced the griffins once more. "Guard Her Majesty's treasure well," she said loudly. "Her happiness, and that of the Folk of the Realm, now depends on you."

She spun around to her troops. "About face! Forward march!" she ordered. And gladly the guards turned and marched away from the fearsome creatures whose stonelike stillness had somehow started to seem even scarier than their growling.

When the guards had rounded the corner, the griffins sat silently for a moment longer. Then in one movement they all lay down. Still they made no sound, but their red eyes were fierce and watchful. They didn't look up as the flower fairies fluttered from their places and flew off. They didn't scratch, or twitch an eyelid, or move a muscle. They just crouched, on guard.

"Mission accomplished," muttered the head guard as she marched her troops past Patrice, Maybelle, Giff and Jessie. "See you back at the palace."

"We did it, we did it!" twittered the fairies,

landing on Jessie's shoulder.

Jessie peeped out at the motionless griffins. "They should be all right from now on, don't you think?" she asked Maybelle.

"I'd say so," replied the little horse. "They look much more normal now. That was quite a good idea of yours. I'm surprised I didn't think of it myself."

"*Quite* a good idea?" exclaimed Patrice. "It was brilliant!" She clapped her hands. "Now I can stock up on food again."

Giff nodded. "Brilliant!" he said. "Now I can get back into my house."

"And I," snuffled Maybelle, "can get a bowl of oats in peace."

"And Jessie," squeaked a tiny voice in Jessie's ear, "can come and dance with us! Can't you, Jessie?"

Jessie giggled as she felt Daffodil's tiny hand plucking at her hair. She raised her arms. She felt her wings billow around her and her feet lift from the ground. "Yes," she laughed. "I can."

67

Jessie would never forget her first dance with the flower fairies of the Realm. In the center of a ring of tall trees, with Violet, Daffodil, Rose, Daisy and Bluebell close beside her and hundreds of other delicate winged creatures moving around her, she floated, spun and swayed to music that seemed to come out of the golden air.

Soaring in the blue between the treetops, or springing on the grassy ground, she danced, for the first time since she was very, very small, without thinking about what she was doing. It was the wings that made the difference, she thought. Because they were making her lighter than air, she could forget all about stumbling or being stiff and shy. The music seemed to become part of her, filling her mind, and making her arms, hands and feet move of their own accord. It was a wonderful feeling.

"That was so lovely!" she sighed to Patrice after the music had finally drifted into silence and the fairies, chattering and waving, had flown back to the trees to rest. "That was . . . I suppose that was just like dancing's supposed to be. Oh, I wish . . .

I wish I could borrow these wings. Just for tonight. I've got to dance at my school concert. The wings would help so much!"

She glanced at the little housekeeper's thoughtful face. "Don't worry, Patrice. I know it's impossible," she added quickly.

Patrice cupped her chin in a small, plump hand and winked. "Nothing's impossible, dearie," she said.

CHAPTER SEVEN

Home—and safe?

"Now, remember, Jessie," fussed Patrice. "You have to return the wings tomorrow morning, first thing. No matter what. They mustn't be out of the Realm for more than a day, or they'll begin to fade and spoil. All right?"

"I'll remember," promised Jessie. Clutching the precious wings, she bent and kissed Patrice on the cheek. "Thank you very much for breaking the rules for me," she said. "I hope you won't get into trouble."

Patrice beamed. "I don't see why I should," she said. "After all, no one knows about it except us."

"Jessie, Jessie!" The familiar trilling calls came closer as Jessie's five fairy helpers sped toward her. They landed, tumbling, in her hair. She laughed and tried to shake them loose.

"You aren't going home, are you?" asked Daffodil. "Not yet."

"Not yet, not yet," chanted the others.

"I have to," cried Jessie. "Now, be good and let me go!" She shook her head again, and Daisy and Bluebell fell bouncing and giggling onto the silken bundle in her arms.

Daisy sat up and looked at the soft mass of shimmering sky blue around her. "Wings!" she shouted in delight. "Jessie's still got her wings!"

"Jessie, will you dance with us again? Please, please?" All the fairies fluttered onto Jessie's fingers and began jumping up and down.

"Oh, shhh! Oh, please be quiet!" begged Jessie in alarm. She glanced at Patrice's horrified face. If the fairies went around spreading the word that she'd borrowed a pair of Queen Helena's wings, she and Patrice would both be in trouble!

Patrice stepped forward and raised her finger.

"It's a *secret* that Jessie is borrowing the wings," she said sternly. "You fairies aren't to say a word to anyone about it. Do you understand?"

The five fairies stared at her, wide-eyed.

"Don't say a word to anyone," Patrice repeated. "Or . . ." She hesitated, searching for a threat that was terrible enough to frighten them into keeping quiet. Then she had an inspiration. "Or Jessie will never be able to dance with you again!" she warned.

The fairies looked at one another. "We won't say anything. We promise!" said Daffodil. All the others nodded solemnly.

"Thank you," said Jessie, looking down at them.

"If we're good, and don't say anything, you *will* dance with us again one day, won't you?" murmured shy little Violet.

Jessie smiled. "Of course I will," she said.

She waved to Patrice and faced the hedge. "Open," she said. She closed her eyes. And then she felt the cool breeze stir her hair and brush her face as she disappeared through the black archway.

Jessie opened her eyes again in the secret garden. The wings were still clutched firmly under one arm. Her heart gave a great thump. She was home. She had the wings. Everything was going to be fine! She shook back her tangled hair and laughed as the tingling flecks of magic clinging there flew into the air.

She ran up to the house. The breakfast things were still on the table but she didn't stop to tidy up. She ran straight to her bedroom and went in, shutting the door behind her. Her butterfly costume—leotard, tights, and the headband that held the silver antennae—lay on the desk by the window. Spread out over them were the blue silk wings Granny had found in her storeroom.

Jessie unrolled the magic wings from the Realm and put them on her bed. She put the other wings beside them. They really did look alike, if you didn't examine them too closely. She didn't think anyone would notice the difference if she wore the Realm pair in the concert tonight.

They'd notice if she flew. But she wouldn't do

that, of course. The Realm wings would just make her graceful and lighter than air, as they had when she danced with the flower fairies. It wasn't really cheating, she told herself. Everyone would be happier if she danced well. Except maybe Irena Bins.

She folded the wings Granny had given her and hid them away on the top shelf of her cupboard. Then, carefully, she spread out the Realm wings on the desk in their place. She peered out the window. Gray clouds were gathering. Perhaps it was going to rain. She pulled the window shut, just in case. She didn't want the wings to get wet.

Feeling very happy, Jessie flung herself down on her bed. She yawned. She realized that she was very tired. No wonder—she'd had a busy morning. She yawned again, and decided to stay where she was for ten minutes. She'd just have a little rest. Mum and Granny wouldn't be home for an hour at least. She closed her eyes and put her hands behind her head. Just ten minutes. Then she'd go and tidy up the kitchen. Ten minutes . . .

But at the end of ten minutes, Jessie was sound asleep, her door and window tightly shut.

So she didn't hear the first sound—the scrabbling and scratching outside among the trees. And she didn't hear the second sound—the tiny voices desperately calling her from the secret garden. And she didn't hear the third, fourth and fifth sounds—Granny's big cat, Flynn, meowing from the kitchen, padding up the corridor toward her room, scratching at her door. Or even the sixth— the beating of the rain on the roof as it tumbled from the gray clouds at last, drenching the flowers and trees and streaming over the ground.

In fact, Jessie was sleeping so deeply that she didn't hear anything at all until Rosemary, her mother, opened her bedroom door an hour later and said, "Jessie, what are you doing sleeping at this hour? Aren't you feeling well?"

"What on earth's the matter with that cat?" Rosemary stared at Flynn, who was sitting by the back door, growling softly.

Flynn turned and blinked. Rosemary heaved two bags of groceries onto the cluttered kitchen table.

"Honestly, Jessie," she said. "I really wish you'd done what I asked and tidied the kitchen for when I came home." She reached over and crossly clapped the lid on the big brown sugar pot.

"Sorry, Mum," said Jessie, rubbing her eyes. She was still a bit dazed with sleep. She seized the sugar pot and took it to the pantry. Then she began to scuttle around putting the other breakfast things away.

Her mother started unpacking the groceries, glancing at her every now and then.

"Are you sure you're feeling all right, Jessie?" she asked, after a moment. "Are you nervous about the concert tonight?"

Jessie turned to her and smiled. "No," she said. "Not anymore."

Rosemary looked at her curiously. "Well, that's good," she said. "I'd started thinking that maybe you . . . oh well, never mind."

"Where's Granny?" Jessie asked.

"She's changing her clothes. She got wet at the shops, running around in the rain like a schoolkid." Rosemary shook her head and grinned. "We met the Bins from next door while we were dashing for the car. They looked at her as though she was crazy. She says it doesn't matter — they've always thought she was. Did you hear the rain, Jessie? It was a real spring storm. Sunshine one minute, heavy rain the next, then sun again. It's beautiful now."

She wandered over to the open kitchen door and looked out, her eyes dreamy. "So peaceful," she said. "So quiet and peaceful." Then her brow wrinkled. She leaned forward. Flynn backed away from the door and hissed.

Jessie's grandmother swept into the kitchen, wearing a long, soft blue dress. The charm bracelet on her arm jingled. Her thick white hair hung in a damp plait down her back. Her cheeks were pink and her green eyes twinkled. "What's Flynn complaining about now?" she laughed.

Rosemary turned around. "I think there's a big animal in the garden, Mum," she said. "Very big. I caught a glimpse of it just now, but then it disappeared behind the trees. Do the Bins have a dog?"

"No." Granny looked surprised.

Rosemary shrugged. "Oh well," she said. "Maybe it was just a shadow."

"Maybe," agreed Granny. But she frowned and went to the back door to look out herself.

A flicker of panic flared up in Jessie's mind. Just a flicker. But then she shook her head. No. There was nothing to worry about. The griffins were in the Realm, guarding the treasure house and Queen Helena's wings. And there was no way they could know that a pair of those wings was here in this house.

Was there?

At lunch, Granny was strangely silent. Flynn sat close to her chair, sometimes patting her ankle with his paw. Jessie's stomach felt upset and jumpy. Something was wrong. She could feel it.

As soon as they had finished clearing away, she ran up to her room again. She sat down on the bed, pressing her hand to her stomach.

"Jessie! Jessie!" A tiny voice sounded faintly in the stillness of the room.

Jessie sat bolt upright and looked wildly

around. But there was nothing to see. The only movement was the fluttering of a butterfly outside the window. She shook her head. She was hearing things. She took some deep breaths and tried to calm down.

"Jessie! Jessie! Jessie!" Now the voice was desperate. Jessie spun around. It was coming from outside!

She jumped up from the bed and ran to the window. A fragile, hovering splash of color danced behind the glass. The butterfly. Then Jessie narrowed her eyes. No!

Quickly she unlatched the windows and pushed them so they swung wide open. The tiny creature fluttered in and landed on her arm.

"Violet!" Jessie blinked at the trembling fairy in astonishment. "What are you doing here?"

"Oh, Jessie, Jessie!" panted Violet. Jessie bent down, straining to hear. It was hard enough to hear the fairy's voice in the Realm, but here it was almost impossible. And her body looked so small! No wonder humans sometimes couldn't tell the difference between fairies and butterflies. Jessie had made the same mistake herself.

"We . . . we came to warn you!" Violet clasped her hands. "The griffins!"

"What?" Jessie jumped. "What about the griffins?"

Violet burst into tears. "We were just talking — about you, and the wings." She sobbed. "You told us not to tell anyone, and we didn't. But we went to play in the red trees, near the treasure house, and we were just talking, and then . . . oh!" She put her face in her hands.

"The griffins heard you saying I had a pair of wings," said Jessie, trying to be calm. "Violet, is that what happened? Is it?"

"Ye-es," wailed Violet. "And the big one growled at the others, and one of them got up and flew off. And then we realized . . ."

"It's here, isn't it?" whispered Jessie. She remembered how Flynn had growled in the kitchen. She licked her lips. Her mouth was dry. "A griffin came through the Door to the Realm. It's looking for the wings."

Violet raised her head and nodded. Her tiny face

was pink and puffy with tears. "We followed it," she hiccuped. "Rose and Daffodil and Daisy and Bluebell and me. We saw it go out of the garden and up to the big trees around your house. We tried to call you, but you didn't hear us. And then . . ."

"Violet, listen," begged Jessie. "Where are the others? Calm down and tell me."

Violet swallowed. "It started to rain," she said. "And we got such a fright. We had to get under shelter, very quickly. That's the rule. Because if our wings get wet, we can't fly. And if we can't fly . . ." She swallowed again. "We panicked," she cried. "We did what they always say not to do. We all flew in different directions, looking for somewhere to hide. I got under a big leaf near the house. Then, when the rain stopped and I came out, I couldn't find the others. I called, and I looked, and I called. But . . ."

"You mean they're lost?" Jessie bit her lip. "You don't think the griffin could have . . . ?"

"Oh no. The griffin wouldn't hurt them," said Violet. "I don't even know where the griffin is, now. It flew off when it started raining. But Jessie, there are so many other dangers here! Cats, and spiderwebs, and deep holes and—and . . . Oh, where are they? Where are they?"

Jessie knew what she had to do. "Get onto my shoulder, Violet," she said. "And don't cry anymore. We're going to find them."

CHAPTER EIGHT

The search

Violet flew to Jessie's shoulder and crouched down among her long red hair. She was so light that Jessie couldn't feel her.

"Here we go, then," said Jessie, leaving the bedroom and shutting the door behind her.

Jessie could just hear the sound of Violet's tiny, panting breaths as she walked into the empty kitchen and toward the back door. She opened it and looked out. There was nothing to be seen but shadows moving on the ground among the tall, dripping trees. Shadows? Or . . .

"Where were you all standing when the rain

started, Violet?" she asked. "What could you see?"

"We were down there, near the entrance to your garden," said Violet's voice in her ear. "We could see through the trees, all the way up here to the house. The door was open. The griffin was coming up this way and we decided we'd have to follow it. Then the rain started. The griffin flew off, over to one side of the garden. The side near the fence." She waved a hand toward Irena Bins' house. "I think Daffodil went the same way, to keep an eye on it. Wait!" She paused. "Someone's calling!" Her voice was excited now.

Jessie listened hard. She couldn't hear anything.

"There it is again!" cried Violet. She tugged gently at Jessie's hair. "Jessie! I think it's Rose! I think she's here, in the house!"

"Rose?" Jessie looked around the tidy kitchen. "But where?"

"She's trapped!" squeaked Violet. "She can't get out. Oh . . . she says it's dark. She's frightened. Oh, Jessie help her!"

Jessie spun around, confused. *Think*, said a voice in her mind. *Don't panic. Think!*

86

Quickly Jessie went over what must have happened. The fairies had been looking up at the house from the secret garden. The back door had been open. Rose could easily have flown straight into the kitchen. No one would have seen her. Mum and Granny were out, and Jessie had been asleep in her bedroom.

Jessie clicked her tongue. If she'd cleaned up the breakfast things earlier, as her mother asked, she'd have seen Rose come in. She would have heard the story then. If only . . .

She gasped. The breakfast things. She had a flash of memory. Her mother, complaining about the mess, leaning over and banging the lid onto the big brown sugar pot. Rose was a plump little fairy. She probably loved sugar.

She rushed to the pantry, with Violet clinging to her hair. She pulled out the sugar pot and lifted the lid . . .

"Rose!" squealed Violet in delight.

Jessie scooped the pale, trembling pink figure from its prison and gently laid it in the palm of her hand. Violet fluttered down from her shoulder and the two fairies clung together.

"I thought you'd never come!" sobbed Rose. "Oh, I was just tasting a little bit of sugar. And then I heard voices, so I crouched down to hide. And then—then . . ." The sob became a wail. "I got locked in. And the lid was so heavy. I couldn't lift it! Oh, I thought you'd never find me! I thought . . ."

"Well, we did find you, Rose," soothed Jessie. "It's all right now." She sounded calmer than she felt. The brown sugar pot was only used in the mornings. Granny put sugar in her tea at breakfast, but the rest of the time she drank it without sugar, like Mum. If Rose hadn't been found, she would certainly have been trapped in the sugar pot all night. And there might not have been enough air in the pot to last that long. Even for a fairy.

Jessie shuddered. "We've got to find the others," she said urgently. "We've got to find them quickly."

She glanced at her watch. It was three o'clock. The concert began in two hours. There were still three fairies to find. And out in the garden the griffin was prowling. It wouldn't hurt the fairies. But Jessie, who had taken a pair of Queen Helena's precious wings, was another matter.

She looked out the back door again. Her feet felt heavy. She didn't want to leave the safety of Blue Moon, but she had no choice. She had a feeling that Daisy, Bluebell and Daffodil were in terrible danger. And she had to find them and help them, before it was too late.

"Get onto my shoulder," she said to Violet and Rose. "We're going outside."

Jessie padded through the wet grass along the side of the house, softly calling the fairies' names.

"I'm sure Bluebell and Daisy are together," Rose snuffled. "I'm sure they flew past me, heading this way."

Where could they be? Jessie peered into the flower beds, rubbed her eyes, peered again. But there was no sign of Daisy and Bluebell, or of Daffodil.

There was no sign of the griffin either. That

was one good thing, at least, thought Jessie. Though in a way she almost wished she *would* see it. Then at least she'd know where it was, instead of expecting it to leap out, screeching, from every bush and dark corner she passed.

"I flew all around the house," Violet piped up from her shoulder. "I called and called, as loudly as I could. But even though the rain had stopped, the water was running along the ground from the front and making a noise, so I suppose they couldn't hear me."

Jessie stopped. Violet was right. When it rained at Blue Moon the water did run down beside the house in streams.

"Hold on!" she said. Then she turned around and hurried back the way she'd come.

In the back garden the big trees still dripped. Jessie ran down among them.

"Jessie, they didn't come this way!" called Rose. But Jessie didn't stop. She knew exactly where she was going. She didn't think about the griffin, or the moving shadows to her right and left. She didn't think about anything except the danger she had suddenly understood.

The land on which Blue Moon was built sloped very slightly downwards, and when it rained water flowed from the front of the house to the back, trickling down into the trees. Jessie's feet splashed now as she ran on the soaked grass. She remembered finding quite deep puddles down at the bottom of the garden many hours after the rain had stopped. When she was little she used to sail leaves in them. Sometimes she would find drowned beetles, moths, butterflies . . .

"Help! Help! Help!"

The little voices were sharp with fear. Jessie's eyes widened, while on her shoulder Rose and Violet began calling and crying in answer.

"There!" shrieked Rose.

And then Jessie saw what Rose's keener eyes had seen before her. Clinging together, on a half-sinking leaf in the middle of a broad brown puddle, were Daisy and Bluebell. Their wings hung wet and useless down their backs. As Jessie watched, the leaf sank lower in the water. All the fairies screamed. Rose and Violet darted from her shoulder. They hovered helplessly over their friends, holding out their arms.

"I'm here," gasped Jessie, falling to her knees beside the puddle. She dipped her hand into the cold water and scooped up Daisy, Bluebell and the leaf in her palm. The two bedraggled fairies rolled off the leaf and lay still, panting, with their eyes closed.

"Take them into the sun!" cried Rose. Cupping the tiny bodies carefully, Jessie did as she was told, running out from among the trees and up to the back door where sunlight still warmed the stone steps. She sat down and opened her hand. The sun beamed down on the pale, wet figures lying there.

"Oh, poor Bluebell! Poor Daisy!" sobbed Violet, kneeling down beside them with Rose and stroking their faces. "Oh, their wings! Look at their wings!"

But Jessie could see that already the warm sun was doing its work. The sad, limp wings were beginning to dry. She sighed with relief. Bluebell and Daisy stirred and opened their eyes. After a moment they sat up. They spread out their wings and began opening and closing them gently.

"What happened?" asked Rose. "How did you fall into the puddle? You nearly drowned!"

"We . . . we made a terrible mistake," croaked Daisy. "We thought we'd be safe and dry close beside the house, under the eaves. And at first we were. Then, suddenly, all this water started running down, right where we were hiding."

"So we held onto the leaf." Bluebell shuddered. "But our wings got wet. And the water pushed us down beside the house, and over the grass, and down to that big puddle. We couldn't let go of the leaf or do anything. And we couldn't fly." Tears rolled down her cheeks.

"Don't cry, Bluebell," begged Violet. "Don't cry. Jessie found you. Just like she found Rose. You're safe."

Daisy sat up straighter. "But the griffin!" she exclaimed. "I'd forgotten. Oh, Jessie, did they tell you about the griffin?"

Violet and Rose nodded. "We don't know where it is," said Rose. Her lip quivered. "And we don't know where . . ." Her voice trailed off.

Daisy stared at her for a moment. Then she twisted around, looking in all directions. "Daffodil!" she cried. "Where's Daffodil?"

CHAPTER NINE

Rescue

They wandered around the garden, calling in low voices, looking everywhere. Jessie trod carefully, her spine prickling, expecting every moment to hear the sound of the griffin. But they saw nothing.

"Daffodil flew that way, toward the fence," said Violet, pointing to the side of the garden. "I'm sure she did."

"We thought so too," chorused Bluebell and Daisy. They had quite recovered now, and were sitting high on Jessie's shoulder with their friends.

"But we've looked all along the fence," said

97

Jessie, glancing at her watch. She was terribly worried about bright, cheeky little Daffodil, and they were running out of time. Soon Mum would be calling her to go and dress for the concert.

"Let's look again. Please, Jessie!" begged Rose.

"Please, please, please," echoed the others.

Jessie sighed. "All right," she said. Again she trudged over to the side fence and began walking along it, looking in every direction and murmuring words of comfort to the fairies on her shoulder.

Suddenly she saw Mr. Bins, Irena's father, staring at her from the back steps of the house next door. Irena was with him, already dressed in her rainbow costume. Jessie wondered how long they'd been there, watching her. They probably wondered what she was doing. Maybe they'd seen her talking to the fairies. If they had, they probably thought she was talking to herself.

She saw Mr. Bins mutter something and Irena giggle, and felt herself beginning to blush with embarrassment. They already thought Granny was crazy. Now they thought she was too.

She turned her head away, and as she did so,

she saw Granny trudging up toward the house from the secret garden, Flynn at her heels. She couldn't see Jessie, hidden among the trees.

How odd, Jessie thought. I was sure Granny was inside. I didn't see her leave the house. She must have come out to the garden while I was around the front. Or even while I was in my room, talking to Violet. But what's she been doing down in the secret garden all this time?

For a moment Jessie thought of calling out to Granny and asking her to help. After all, Granny came from the Realm herself. And Jessie knew she had great powers. If anyone could find Daffodil, she could.

But as her grandmother came closer, Jessie realized she couldn't ask her. She was plodding rather than walking, looking neither right nor left. A fairy Queen she might be, but just now she looked small, frail, and terribly tired. She must have stayed out in the garden too long. After all, she had been ill and she was only just getting better.

Jessie walked on, trailing her hand along the

fence. A brown-and-orange speckled butterfly flew past her nose. Keep away from the Bins' house, butterfly, she warned it silently. You're a pretty one. Irena might decide she wants you for her picture frame.

Then she stopped and gasped aloud, gripping the fence so hard that her hand hurt.

"What's the matter?" cried the fairies on her shoulder. "Jessie! What's the matter?"

Jessie could hardly speak. Her teeth had started chattering with shock and fear. Suddenly she knew where Daffodil was. She knew it without a shadow of a doubt.

"I think . . ." she began. She swallowed, and began again. "I think the girl who lives next door might have mistaken Daffodil for a butterfly. I think she might have caught her, and taken her inside."

The fairies whispered together excitedly while Jessie pressed her lips together, trying not to panic. They didn't know what she knew about Irena and her butterflies. They didn't know that Daffodil was in terrible danger. They didn't know how hard it was going to be to save her — or that, even now, it might be too late. She peered through the fence. Irena would never let her just go in and take Daffodil. Even if she believed she was a fairy. *Especially* if she believed she was a fairy.

She made up her mind. There was no time to lose. "Wait here," she ordered. "Stay out of sight. I'm going to get Daffodil."

The fairies flew up into a tree and clustered together, holding one another's hands. "Good luck, Jessie," called Violet in a small voice.

Jessie crawled over the fence and crept up the path that ran along the side of the Bins' house. Several windows were open, but she didn't know where Irena's room was. She'd just have to get into the house and hope for the best.

She pulled herself up so that she could look into the first room she came to. It seemed to be a spare bedroom. Without really thinking what she was doing, she scrambled up and over the sill.

"Mum!" Irena's voice sounded piercingly just outside the room. Jessie's heart thudded. She scuttled over to hide herself behind the door.

"Mum, aren't you ready yet?" Irena demanded. "I want to go! I want to be early! I want to get there before that stupid Jessie does, or Ms. Hewson will be fussing over her as usual and won't have time to watch me practice my dance."

"All right, Irena, all right," called Mrs. Bins. Jessie heard her footsteps coming closer. "Dad's just getting the car. We've got plenty of time."

"Just come *on*!" snapped Irena's voice.

Jessie sighed with relief as the two sets of footsteps tapped away from the spare room and toward the back door. As it opened, Jessie heard her own mother's voice calling her.

"There, you see?" said Mrs. Bins. "Jessie's mother is only just calling her to get dressed. My goodness, they're cutting it fine, aren't they?"

Irena laughed unpleasantly. "Jessie's probably hiding," she sniggered. "Too scared to turn up at the concert. You'd feel the same if you danced like her."

The back door slammed shut. Jessie stood for a moment in the spare room, holding her breath. She was hot all over. What a horrible girl Irena Bins was!

She crept out into the short hallway that led to the front of the house. Irena's room must surely be up this way, she thought.

She was right. "Irena sleeps here," said the painted china notice on the white door next to the bathroom. Jessie pushed open the door and switched on the light.

There was the picture Sal had described. Irena in a beautiful butterfly costume, pink-and-silver wings outstretched. And all around the picture were butterflies, pinned to a board. Blue wings, orange-and-brown wings, blue-and-black wings. But, thank goodness, no bright yellow wings. Not yet. Jessie shuddered. Once she'd found a dead butterfly and taken it home. And once she'd seen a real butterfly collection in a museum. But how could *anyone* kill such beautiful things just to make a *picture frame*?

She spun around, searching desperately. And then her heart leaped. There, on a shelf, was a big jar. And fluttering weakly inside it, her tiny hands beating on the glass, was Daffodil. With a cry Jessie ran to the shelf, lifted down the jar and unscrewed the lid. "Daffodil," she breathed, tears springing into her eyes. "Oh, poor Daffodil."

She lowered her hand into the jar and Daffodil fell, exhausted, onto her fingers. Gently and carefully Jessie lifted her out. She could see that the little fairy was bruised all over.

"The human girl caught me in a net!" Daffodil cried. "After the rain. I could hardly breathe, in the jar. Oh, Jessie . . ."

"You're all right now, Daffodil," said Jessie grimly. She had never been so furious with anyone as she was with Irena Bins at the moment. "Come on. I'm taking you home." Holding Daffodil carefully, she ran to the window and began to climb out.

"The others . . . are the others all right?" called Daffodil. "And, Jessie, the griffin!"

"It's all right," soothed Jessie. "Everything's fine. Don't worry. Don't worry about anything."

She jumped down onto the path at the side of the house.

"Jessie! Jessie!" Mum was still calling. Jessie glanced at her watch again. Ten minutes to five!

And she wasn't even dressed. No wonder Mum sounded so desperate!

She raced down to the tree where the other fairies were waiting. They screamed with joy when they saw Daffodil, and flew to Jessie's shoulders like tiny birds. Still cradling Daffodil in her hand, Jessie ran for the secret garden.

She was late. She was terribly late. She was so late that Ms. Hewson would probably be very angry with her. She was so late that they might even start the concert without her, and let Irena dance in her place. And then Irena would be so triumphant! And Jessie would never have the chance to show her, and everyone else, just how well she could dance—if she had the right wings.

But it didn't matter. Nothing mattered except that all the fairies were alive and happy.

As she ran back up to the house to face her mother's worried, angry face, and then the crazy quick change in her bedroom and the terrible rush in the car to school, Jessie knew that she wouldn't have missed the chance of helping them for anything in the world.

CHAPTER TEN

The Butterfly

S al, golden in her sun costume, her spiky head-dress standing out all around her worried face, was hovering by the concert hall entrance as Jessie, Rosemary and Granny rushed from the car. "Jessie, where have you been?" she shouted. "Ms. Hewson's having fits!"

"I'm not surprised," snapped Rosemary. "Jessie, you've got mud on your face!" She dabbed at Jessie's cheeks with a tissue. "Goodness me, you're a mess! Couldn't you have cleaned yourself up a bit? No one asked you to change in the dark! Two seconds to turn on the light wouldn't have made a bit of difference."

Jessie didn't bother to answer. She just stood, panting, while her mother finished cleaning her face and quickly brushed her hair.

"Come on!" yelled Sal. "Everyone's on stage waiting!"

Jessie ran. "Good luck!" Rosemary shouted after her. Jessie raised her hand in reply, and the silk of her wings rustled. She smiled. She didn't need luck.

"Jessie!" shouted the class, as she and Sal came bursting through the side curtains and onto the stage.

"Shhh!" ordered Ms. Hewson. Her curly hair was practically standing on end. "Never do that to me again, Jessica!" she scolded. "I've aged ten years waiting here for you."

"She was trying to get out of coming, I'll bet," Irena Bins said loudly from the back of the stage. "I'll bet her mum made her."

"That's enough, Irena!" Ms. Hewson shot Irena a very unfriendly look. Then she looked at her watch. "It's time," she said. "Places, please. Good luck, everyone. And Jessie—just feel the music."

Jessie went behind the curtains at the side of the stage and waited. She heard the hum of talk from the audience in the concert hall die down as the lights were dimmed. She heard the music begin. She saw the curtains open. She saw Sal standing at the back of the stage, her arms outstretched. She saw the kids who were playing flowers swaying in time with the music. Soon the tune would swell and change, and then it would be her turn to go on. Mum and Granny would be watching her. All those hundreds of people would be watching her. Fear jabbed at her stomach.

She heard her music begin, and the old, awful, scared feeling turned her body to ice. Stiffly she raised her arms. Then she felt the silken blue wings float around her shoulders and down her back. At once the memories of her dance in the Realm came flooding back to her. The trees, the music, the golden air. Daffodil, Daisy, Bluebell, Rose and shy little Violet.

Jessie smiled. She ran onto the stage. Her wings

fluttered under the light. She swayed and turned. She was lighter than air. It was as if the music was part of her. She danced as she had danced with the fairies in the Realm. And she loved it.

Ms. Hewson watched from her place offstage. She tugged at her curly hair. She couldn't believe her eyes. But by the time the play was a quarter of the way through, her face was aching with smiling.

At the end, the audience clapped and cheered wildly. They clapped the sun, and the rainbow, and the flowers. They clapped the breeze, and the clouds, and the rabbits, and Ms. Hewson. But the longest claps, the loudest cheers, were for Jessie.

Jessie collapsed into the car, her head in a happy whirl of excitement.

"You were really marvelous, Jessie," said Rosemary, as they started home. "I had no idea you could dance like that. Had you, Mum?"

"I knew Jessie would be fine," said Granny mildly. "Once she learned to forget herself and just let the music lead her."

In the back seat, Jessie wriggled a bit uncomfortably. They wouldn't feel so proud of her if they knew about the borrowed wings.

Rosemary laughed. "I didn't think we'd make it," she said. "I really didn't. What on earth were you *doing* to make you so late, Jessie?"

Jessie shrugged in the darkness. "Mucking around," she said. "I, um, just ran out of time." That was true, anyway, she thought.

"Well, I must say you were very casual about the whole thing," said Rosemary. "I thought at least you'd have put out your costume ready to slip on."

Jessie sat forward. The car hummed along the road. "I did," she said.

Her mother shook her head. "Oh no you didn't," she said. "You'd started, but you'd forgotten the wings. When I went into your room, there were the leotard and tights and headband on the desk, and the window gaping wide open, and no wings! The wings were still in your cupboard. I had to get them out for you. They were up really high too. I nearly didn't see them."

Jessie's mouth fell open. Shocked, she peered closely at the blue silk wing dangling from her wrist. Her stomach turned over. She felt the edge of the silk with her fingers. Neat machine stitching. She gasped. These weren't the Realm wings. These were . . .

Granny gave a low, musical laugh. "Those wings looked pretty on you years ago, Rosemary, and tonight they looked just as pretty on Jessie," she said. "They've done good service."

Jessie slumped back against the car seat. She couldn't believe what she was hearing.

"I danced well," she said finally, in a small voice. "And I did it myself."

Rosemary laughed again. "So we've been telling you," she said. "Haven't you had enough praise for one night?"

"I think she's just realized what it all means," said Granny, smiling in the darkness and smothering a yawn.

Rosemary looked at her curiously. "And could I ask what you were doing this afternoon, Mum, to make you so terribly tired? You should take it easy, you know."

Granny inspected her charm bracelet. "As you

suspected, Rosemary, there was a rather large . . . ah . . . creature in the garden. I decided it would be best to send it home."

Jessie clapped her hand over her mouth to stop herself from squealing.

Now it was Rosemary's turn to be surprised. "Mum, why didn't you tell me?" she demanded. "Jessie could have done that for you." She swung the car into the Blue Moon driveway.

Granny shook her head. "Oh no," she said. "Jessie had a few other little problems on her mind. Five of them, I think. And the creature . . . knows me. Besides, it had what it wanted from the house, thanks to an open window. There was no point in it remaining. I simply told it so, and—after a bit of an argument—off it went." She turned around and winked at Jessie.

"You mean some animal's been in the house?" Rosemary exploded. She pulled the car up in front of the garage and sat behind the steering wheel, shaking her head. "What next! How can you take these things so calmly, Mum?"

Granny opened the car door. Her charm

bracelet jingled on her wrist. "I take things as I find them," she said. "I move with the music, like Jessie. I find that's always the best way."

Jessie couldn't wait to get inside the house. She had to think. She ran to her room to change, her head spinning. The griffin had stolen back the magic wings from her room while she was helping the fairies. Granny and Flynn had sent the griffin home, and it had taken the wings with it. Mum had put out the old wings, and Jessie had hurriedly put them on in the dimness of her room without noticing the difference. She had danced in wings that were no more magic than her black leotard. And Granny had known, all the time.

Jessie went to her window. Mum had left it slightly open so that the soft evening breeze came through. Soon the moon would be rising. And Daffodil, Rose, Daisy, Bluebell and Violet were safe at home again.

"Goodnight, little fairies," Jessie said. Then she saw something lying on the desk just beside the window. A small scrap of gold silk tied with silver thread. There was something hard inside. She unrolled the silk carefully. A golden butterfly slid into her hand. Another Realm charm for her bracelet. And there was a note. *Thank you, Jessie,* the note read. *We'll always remember.*

Jessie sat down and fixed the golden butterfly to her bracelet, beside the heart that already hung there.

She looked out the window again. "And thank you," she whispered.

The bracelet tinkled as she took off her blue silk wings and slipped the silver headband from her hair. The concert was over and so was this amazing day. But in her mind Jessie could still hear music. She could still hear the fairies laughing, the screeching of the griffin, Patrice's chatter, Giff's wails and bossy Maybelle giving orders. She could still see the ring of tall trees, the golden air, the cloud of fairies dancing against the blue sky, the shimmering wings spread out on a yellow silk bedcover. She could still feel the tiny weight of the flower fairies on her shoulder. The glorious feeling of flying.

She looked at the bracelet again. The fairies were right. They would always remember today, and so would she. This had been the kind of day that no one could *ever* forget.

Turn the page for a peek at
Jessie's next adventure in the

FairyRealm:

BOOK 3

The Third wish

Usually Jessie felt peaceful as soon as she entered the secret garden. It was as though the tall hedge kept the whole world out. But today the smell of smoke mingled with the scent of rosemary. Today the air was filled with fear.

"Now," Granny said. "The first thing you must do is go to the palace. You'll need help to get to the Bay."

Jessie nodded. Her friend, Patrice, was the housekeeper at the palace. Patrice was always glad to see her. And perhaps Maybelle, the bossy miniature horse, and Giff the elf would be there too. They would help her. She knew they would.

"Be back by afternoon-tea time," Granny warned. "No later." She looked up at the hazy sky. "The fires are getting closer," she murmured.

She spun round to face Jessie. "All right," she said. "Go! Go quickly!"

She held up her hand. "Open!" she commanded.

Jessie heard the familiar rushing sound as the Door began to open. She closed her eyes and felt the cool breeze surround her, lifting her long red hair off her shoulders and blowing it around her head.

Then suddenly she remembered something.

"Granny," she called. "If the wish-stones are the second most powerful wish-granters in the Realm, what's the first?"

With the sound of the opening Door filling her ears and her mind, she struggled to hear Granny's answer. It could be important. If she couldn't find a wish-stone, maybe she could dare to go to the most powerful wish-granter of all to get the fires stopped.

But when Granny's answer came, sounding small and far away, she was very surprised.

"Magic fish," Granny called.

Fish? Had Granny really said "fish"?

Jessie strained her ears to hear over the rising and falling of the wind. "Magic fish," cried Granny's voice. "But don't . . . magic fish . . . rules . . . Under-Sea . . . no use . . ."

Then her voice disappeared completely, and Jessie was whirling away.

Into the Realm.

EMILY RODDA

has written many books for children,
including the Rowan of Rin books.
She has won the Children's Book
Council of Australia Book of the
Year Award an unprecedented five
times. A former editor, Ms. Rodda is
also the best-selling author of adult
mysteries under the name Jennifer
Rowe. She lives in Australia.